Hi! READ, STICK & LEARN
about
ANIMALS

Animals are different colors: **blue,** **red,** **yellow,** **reddish,**

crowned pigeon   cardinal bird   duckling   red fox

brown, **pink,** **green,** **gray,**

brown bear   sow   green grasshopper   elephant

black, white or **black and white** and even **multicolored !**

giant panda   macaw

There are blue animals…

The crowned pigeon lives in the islands of the Pacific Ocean.
It makes its nest in the forest and eats the fruit that has fallen from trees.
It is a very strange bird: it flies little, only when it must return to the nest after having
slept on the branches of the trees or when it must find shelter from enemies.
During the mating season, the male displays its
fan-like beautiful feather crest to allure the female.
The female lays just one egg and will hatch it in a big nest.
Both parents will feed their chick.

starfish

common blue

blue macaw

blue rock thrush

crowned pigeon

... red ...

What is red, has a thick beak, a little crest
and lives in North America and in Mexico?
It's the cardinal bird. Have you noticed its cone-shaped beak?
The cardinal bird uses its little beak to break the seeds it eats.
This is why we say it is a granivorous.
The feathers of the female are brown and the male's feathers are bright red.
The mother bird builds the nest for her babies.
After the baby chicks hatch from their eggs, both parents feed them.

blood red cymothoe
butterfly

cardinal bird

common octopus

seven-spot
ladybug

red ibis

red dragonfly

red toad

... yellow ...

The duckling is the chick of the duck and the drake.
It hatches from its egg by using its beak to break the eggshell.
Right after hatching, the duckling already has its eyes open.
Did you know that the duckling leaves the nest as soon as it comes out of its egg?
It can already walk and swim with its webbed feet!
Little, light feathers called down cover its body.
When the duckling grows up, real feathers will take the place of the down.
The feathers will help it to fly.

canary bird

golden weaver

scorpion

chick

sulphur beetle

duckling

brimstone butterfly

... reddish ...

Did you know that the red fox is a very shy animal? It lives in the countryside, in the forest and at the edge of the cities, but it is rather difficult to meet it. Its house is called a den and is dug under the ground. Inside the den, the female gives birth to her cubs during spring. The fox is very active at night or at sunset and has its own way of hunting. When hunting rodents, it lies in wait without moving. As soon as it sees its prey, it attacks by jumping suddenly in the air and falling on the prey's back, the four legs joined. That's it! The prey is stuck with no chance to escape. After having killed its prey, the fox takes it to a hiding place. In case of need, the fox will exactly remember where she left the food supplies.

soldier beetle

kiwi

kinkajou

red fox

golden lion tamarin

red squirrel

orangutan

red salamander

platypus

magpie

white swan

mouse

sulphur beetle

blood red cymothoe butterfly

stag

bee-eaters

earthworm

red-eyed
tree frog

sow

red squirrel

dolphin

red salamander

chick

elephant

gorilla

common
blue

canary bird

American bison

common octopus

soldier beetle

moth

silverfish (insect)

koala

rainbow lorikeet

duckling

tarantula

blue rock thrush

orangutan

Commerson's dolphin

angelfish

red ibis

starfish

scorpion

wild boar

Temminck's trapopan

elk

pink flamingo

green stink bug

green mamba

praying mantis

giant panda

crowned pigeon

slender loris

swallow-tanager

cardinal bird

brimstone butterfly

green grasshopper

green June beetle

green hairstreak

red dragonfly

walrus

Lady Amherst's Pheasant

kiwi

otter

... brown ...

Did you recognize it? It resembles a little teddy bear. It is the brown bear.
It lives in the forests and in the mountains. Don't let its slow heavy walk trick you!
The brown bear can run very fast, can climb the trees, swim, stand up and walk
on its hind legs. During winter, it goes inside a shelter that is dug partly under the
ground, called a den. The bear falls into a special sleep, protected against the cold.
We call this special sleep hibernation. While she hibernates,
the mother bear gives birth to one or two cubs! Cubs are baby bears.
The little bears will get out of the den only after it gets warm outside.

elk

bat

stag

American bison

moth

brown bear

beaver

otter

wild boar

tarantula

platypus

coati

slender
loris

... pink ...

The pig is a domestic animal as compared to its ancestor, the wild boar,
which has remained a wild animal.
Just like man, the pig can eat anything: this is why we say it is an omnivorous animal.
Look attentively at its muzzle! It finishes with a snout with which
the pig routs in the ground looking for food. The pig has a very good sense of smell.
The sow can give birth to about twelve little pigs, which we call piglets.
While they are young, the piglets suckle milk from their mother.
Each of them chooses a teat that will keep it fed until it is able to find food all alone.

pink flamingo

Leadbeater cockatoo

walrus

sow

earthworm

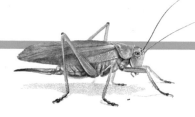

... green ...

In summer, what insect do you meet in the country meadows?
It's the green grasshopper. The male and the female are almost the same.
What is different? The female has a little sword in the upper side of her body.
But don't be afraid! This sword cannot cut or sting.
The grasshopper uses it to bury her eggs under the ground.
The male makes a loud sound by rubbing its wings together.
The grasshoppers have ears on their hind legs under their knees.
What a strange place for ears!

green mamba

green stink bug

Scarce Bamboo
Page

red-eyed tree frog

green grasshopper

swallow-tanager female

praying
mantis

green
hairstreak

basilisk lizard

green June beetle

... gray ...

The African elephant generally lives in a herd. It uses its large ears as fans.
It defends itself and digs the ground with its tusks. It uses its trunk to breathe and smell,
just as we use our nose. The elephant sucks up water with its trunk and blows it into its
mouth to drink, or in the air, above the head, to cool itself. It also uses the trunk
to communicate with the others, or to caress or comfort its cub.
The end of the trunk is like a hand. Therefore, the elephant can dig out grass,
pick up leaves or scratch its back with a branch. That's very practical, isn't it?
The elephant is an herbivorous animal.

koala

mouse

cat

domestic
donkey

silverfish
(insect)

dolphin

rock dove

elephant

... black, white or black and white ...

The giant panda lives in the forests of southeast China. It does not need a den
because its tick, oily fur protects it against cold and rainy weather.
When born, the panda cub is blind, has no teeth and is covered by a thin down.
It nestles in the warm fur of its mother.
After three weeks, the cub starts to look like its parents. For the first four months,
the mother panda carries the cub with her all the time-on her back paw!
At six months old, the cub can walk alone.
Panda bears like to live alone, and they are very quiet.
They eat only plants, especially bamboo.
Panda bears have six fingers on their back paws,
and thcsc hclp them hold the bamboo stems.

Commerson's dolphin

white swan

black panther

gorilla

giant panda

magpie

polar bear